MY HAPPY LIFE

First American edition published in 2013 by Gecko Press USA, an imprint of Gecko Press Ltd.
Reprinted 2013 (twice)

A catalog record for this book is available from the US Library of Congress.

Distributed in the United States and Canada by
Lerner Publishing Group, Inc.
241 First Avenue North
Minneapolis, MN 55401 USA
www.lernerbooks.com

This edition first published in 2012 by Gecko Press
PO Box 9335, Marion Square, Wellington 6141, New Zealand
info@geckopress.com

First published in Sweden by Bonnier Carlsen Bokförlaget, Stockholm, Sweden
Published in the English language by arrangement with Bonnier Carlsen Bokförlaget
Original title: Mitt Lyckliga Liv

Text © Rose Lagercrantz 2010
Illustrations © Eva Eriksson 2010
English language edition © Gecko Press Ltd 2012

Translated by Julia Marshall
Edited by Penelope Todd
Typesetting by Luke Kelly, New Zealand
Printed by Everbest, China

Gecko Press gratefully acknowledges the assistance of Svenska Institutet (SI).

ISBN hardback 978-1-877579-35-6

For more curiously good books, visit www.geckopress.com

My Happy Life

WRITTEN BY

Rose Lagercrantz

ILLUSTRATED BY

Eva Eriksson

GECKO PRESS

CONTENTS

Chapter 1

It was late, but Dani couldn't sleep.

Some people counted sheep, but not her!

Dani counted all the times she'd been happy.

Like the time when she was little and her cousin
Sven gave her a frog.

8

And the first time she managed to swim three
strokes without drowning.

And when she got her new schoolbag.

She was so excited. She'd waited her whole life to start school.

The summer had been very long because she was waiting so hard.

Chapter 2

But when Dani was finally on her way to school,
she started to wonder what would happen.

Would she just sit there and learn to read and write?

She could do that already. A bit, at least. She'd learned at preschool.

"Do you think I'll like my teacher?" she asked her father.

"Of course," he said. "Of course you will."

"Do you think I'll like the other children?"

Dani had been to preschool somewhere else, so she didn't know anybody at the new school.

Suddenly she was scared.

What if she made no friends?

If that happened, she wouldn't ever go back. Definitely not.

"Keep your fingers crossed, Dad!" she said as they went through the gate.

Chapter 3

The teacher was waiting in the classroom to say hello.

One boy refused to go in.

His mother had to bribe him with money.

When everyone was seated, the teacher said, "Welcome to your first day at school!"

Then she called out their names one by one.

Those who were brave enough raised their hands and said, "Yes." Dani raised hers, even though she thought she might faint.

Then they were given pencils and paper to write their names.

Dani's real name was Daniela, but she wrote "Dani."

A girl called Michaela wrote "Mickey."

A boy called Eric wrote "Meatball."

Jonathan just wrote "Jonathan."

Everyone could write their own name except one boy. But the teacher helped him.

Just when it started to be fun, it was time to go home.

That evening, Dani's family celebrated her
first day.

Dani's family was Dani, her father, and Cat.

Cat probably thought that Dani was grown up
now that she had started school.

"It wasn't so hard," she explained to him.
"Maybe a little bit scary, but lots of fun!"

But she didn't have any friends yet.

Chapter 4

The next day, Dani stood alone on the playground. She was all by herself, just watching, for the whole of the first recess.

During the second recess, she noticed another
girl by herself. She was just watching, too.

At exactly the same moment, they looked at each other.

Dani got up the courage to go and ask, "Shall we play on the swings?"

Ella nodded. That was her name.

They played on the swings until the bell rang.
They played on them through all the other
recesses, too.

When school was finished, they wanted to
keep swinging.

They never wanted to stop.

In the end their teacher came and said they had to.

"You can play on the swings tomorrow," she said.

And so they went home—after
many ifs and buts.

Chapter 5

Dani was happy at school.

She was happy when she played on the swings with Ella.

And when they sat in the cozy corner, painting sunsets.

They both loved sunsets.

Dani was happy when the teacher said that she and Ella could sit next to each other.

Only one thing about school was boring: there was no homework.

"Not in the first week," said the teacher.

But Dani wanted homework so badly that her father had to make some for her.

She was happy when the teacher said she could
sit next to Ella at lunchtime as well.

They always ate the same number of
sandwiches for lunch.

Dani ate triangles and Ella ate rectangles.

When they had to find a partner for games, they chose each other, of course.

And they chose each other when they went on a trip to the lookout. First they looked at the view. Then they ate their lunches. And then Ella took out The Surprise.

It was a box with two necklaces inside it, two halves of a heart.

"It's called a friendship necklace," said Ella.

They put on the necklaces and Dani was happy. She was so happy!

She was happy when she went to Ella's house and played with Ella's hamster called Partyboy.

And with her little sister, Miranda.

"Buff!" screamed Miranda when she was angry with them.

She meant enough. But she thought it was buff!

Chapter 6

Dani was happy when Ella was allowed to come and stay the night at her house.

They started the Night Club.

That's a club that starts at ten o'clock and goes on all night.

You talk and shine the flashlight on the ceiling and have a midnight feast of cheese-and-cucumber sandwiches.

When you can't stay awake any longer, you rub each others' backs until you fall asleep.

Dani was happy each time they had NC.

NC is short for Night Club.

She was also happy when she went with Ella to
the pet shop where Partyboy came from.

There were two other very cute, snow-white
hamsters.

Dani and Ella decided that one should be called
Snow and the other one Flake.

"Ask your father if you can buy them," said Ella.

When Dani asked her father, he didn't answer.

It was the worst feeling: when Dani would ask her father something, and he didn't answer.

She was very sad.

But a few minutes later, she was happy again. Or maybe it was hours—a few hours later, probably. Or even days.

She couldn't remember because she was happy so often back then.

She was happy when Ella asked if she wanted to swap bookmarks.

Dani could have any bookmark she wanted, except for one. It was an angel that belonged to Ella's grandma when she was little.

Dani offered her two bookmarks for it, but Ella said no.

She offered three, four, five! She offered all the bookmarks she had.

But Ella refused to swap the angel.

They even stopped being friends because of it.

That happened sometimes.
Not being friends.

But not for long. They usually made up after a
minute or two.

You couldn't find a better friend than Ella. She
and Dani stuck together through wet and dry,
sun and rain, thick and thin.

Chapter 7

They had a fruit week and a vegetable week.
They learned all about fruit and vegetables.

And then it was Christmas.

At Christmas, Dani visited her grandma and grandpa with her father and Cat. She opened presents.

But after she had opened them all and played with them—especially the fluffy polar bear—she started to miss Ella.

Dani was happy when school started again.

They had milk and butter and cheese weeks.

One day they drew cows.

Dani drew a red cow with big horns.

Ella didn't draw anything. She sat with her hands over her eyes.

"What's the matter?" whispered Dani. "Are you crying?"

Ella didn't answer.

The teacher had to explain.

Ella was moving away.

When Dani heard that, she started to cry, too.
She cried and cried.

But what could she do?

Chapter 8

Dani lay in bed counting all the times she'd been happy. But sometimes things had gone wrong.

When Ella stopped coming to school, Dani wasn't happy.

She was unhappy.

She wished she could move, too.
But she had to stay behind.

On the street where she had
lived all her life.
    With her father and Cat.
    In the yellow house.
    The one closest to the park.

Dani used to have a mother who lived there too,
but she had passed away.

That's what people said when someone died.

They said she had passed away, but how could
a dead person pass anything?

And away to where?

Now Ella had gone, too. But she hadn't passed away.

She had gone in a car to another town.

Her town was thousands of streets and roads away from Dani's.

And many thousand forests and streams and hills and lakes…

Beyond the thousands of forests and streams and hills and lakes was where Dani's best friend Ella lived now.

Chapter 9

The day after Ella moved, Dani just sat and stared at the empty chair.

The same day, she fell down on the playground
and tore her tights and hurt her knee.

It hurt so much she thought she would never forget it.

Not until she was thirty-five or even older.

The bandage that her teacher put on didn't
help. It was very small and kept falling off.

Dani kept on crying.

She cried because it hurt.

She cried because
Ella had moved.

Chapter 10

She cried the next day as well.

That was when they played soccer…

...and Jonathan tackled her so hard

that she fell and hurt her head.

Her father had to take her to the doctor
where they stitched up the hole and put on a
big bandage.

But that wasn't why she was crying.

She cried because she wasn't happy any more.

Chapter 11

They had bread week and learned all about bread.
But nothing was fun.

Then one day Dani was walking
home with her father, and he
asked if she still wanted
those hamsters.

   And she was actually
a little bit happy.

   But what if they
were already sold?

When they came to the pet shop, she rushed to
the hamster cage.

Snow and Flake were still there. And they were
just as lovely and cute as they were the first time
Dani saw them.

The shopkeeper put them into a box and gave
it to Dani.

Her father bought a cage, two hamster houses, some vitamins, sawdust, hay, two water bottles, and two food containers.

When they got home, Dani made the cage nice, then Snow and Flake went into their hamster houses and turned their backs.

That's what hamsters do when they want to be left alone.

When they're angry, they grind their teeth.

When they're happy, their eyes sparkle and they make a rumbling noise.

When they're scared, they squeak. And poop.

Actually, they poop the whole time, whether they're scared or not.

Chapter 12

Dani was probably the happiest person she knew but not all the time. She wasn't very happy at recess after Ella moved.

She sat in the corner watching the boys who
were building a city of blocks and Legos.
They kept making it for several days.

None of the girls were allowed to join in.
That made them angry.

When the city was finally finished, the girl
called Mickey knocked over a tower.

And a girl called Vicky bumped a castle.

And suddenly Dani stood up—imagine!
She went and sat right in the middle of the city.

You could say that really brought the house down.

The boys shrieked and started throwing blocks at the girls.

The girls threw them back.

And they all started shoving each other!

Dani shoved Jonathan so hard that he fell and hit his face on the floor.

Blood poured out.

The teacher rushed in. At first she thought it was a bleeding nose, but then she saw that Jonathan's new front teeth had come loose and were going to fall out.

"Run and get the nurse!" she told Vicky and Mickey.

Dani didn't know what happened after that. She didn't dare look.

She was so scared that she hid under the table.

Chapter 13

After that, Dani wasn't happy
for a single moment.

That evening, her father
went to a party and Dani's
grandma came to babysit.

Normally that would make Dani as happy as anything.

Her grandma was wonderful, and she cooked the best food in the world.

She made Dani's favorite dinner—macaroni and tomato sauce.

But that evening, Dani couldn't eat one bite.

All she could think about was how she'd pushed Jonathan and he'd almost lost his front teeth.

It wasn't until they started watching a movie that Dani forgot about it for a moment. She took a gulp of water from a glass on the table.

She felt something hard on her lips. Grandma's false teeth!

Grandma often took them out because they rubbed.

Then Dani couldn't think about anything except false teeth.

What if Jonathan had to have them now?

It would be her fault!

What could she do?

In the end, she decided to write him a letter.

She wrote:

Hi Jonathan!

I didn't mean to push so hard.

I'm sorry.

From Dani

PS If you get false teeth and they rub, you can take them out and put them in a glass of water.

Chapter 14

The next day Dani tried to give the letter to Jonathan.

But he wasn't interested.

He had braces and a new bike. A BMX.

You got on a BMX as if it was a horse.

Otherwise there was nothing special about that sort of bike. It didn't even have a basket.

Soon Jonathan put it down and started
playing marbles.

Again, Dani tried to give him the letter.

He waited until he'd won three times before he read it.

He nodded to Dani. "I won't need false teeth."

Then at last Dani was happy again.

When Mickey and Vicky shouted to Dani to
come and jump rope, she was even happier.
Jump rope was one of her specialties.

That day she managed to do five hundred jumps.
Her whole class stood and watched.

Chapter 15

They had potato week and learned all about potatoes.

And once, after school, Dani went with Vicky and Mickey to look for empty cans and bottles.

They found a lot.

They took them to the recycling center and bought chewing gum with the money.

Dani and Jonathan started a competition to see who had the most stickers, the ones you find on apples and bananas.

They put them under the red mat in the cozy room.

Chapter 16

At school, Dani started every day by writing in her storybook.

Her book was called:

MY HAPPY LIFE

This is what was in it:

My name is Daniela but I am called Dani.
I have blonde hair, yellowy-gold. Light yellowy-gold.
My eyes are blue. My favorite dinner is macaroni
and tomato sauce, and I have been happy many
times in my life.

That's as far as she got.

But everything in the
story was true.

When she was little,
she was happy about
almost everything.

Happy because she had fingers and toes.

She thought her feet
were adorable.

She liked her
tummy as well.
It was so lovely
and soft.
And she had
her mother.

Then her mother got sick and had to go to hospital.

Sometimes she came home. She spent her time on the veranda, resting.

Dani stayed with Grandma and Grandpa a lot.

One day her father called from the hospital and said that her mother had passed away.

Dani was so little, she didn't understand what that meant.

Then her grandma explained that it was just something people say.

Her mother hadn't passed away. She'd gotten wings and flown.

Chapter 17

Her father flew, too, but he flew in a plane. To Italy.

And Dani always went with him because that was where her other grandma lived.

They flew there every summer.

What she remembered best from all her journeys was the time she sat on the baggage cart…

She sat right on top of a pile of suitcases.

Of course, the pile toppled over, but her father rushed up and caught her.

He rescued her all the time.

She wouldn't manage without him.

She was so lucky to have her father.

Another time in Italy, she fell and scraped her hands, her knees, and her nose.

They were at a restaurant.

Everyone at the restaurant was so sorry for her
that they gave her a whole chocolate cake.
Dani shared it with her family.

After that, she and her cousin Alessandro
played together until they were tired, and then
they sat down and talked.

Dani usually spoke English and Alessandro
spoke Italian.

"Fiore," said Alessandro. That meant flower.

Then he said, "Amore." That meant love.

It was a word Dani knew well because her
father said it all the time.

Chapter 18

"Amore," said her father when he popped in to
see her one night. "Aren't you asleep yet?"

"No," said Dani. "I can't."

She usually went to sleep as soon as she put her head on the pillow, but that night she couldn't sleep a wink.

"What shall we do?" Her father was worried. "Are you hungry?"

"Yes," said Dani. "I think I am."

She had heard that there were children who needed food at night. She might be one of those.

She drank some warm milk with honey.

Snow and Flake were also awake, looking at her.

They were probably wondering what was going to happen.

"Amore," she whispered to Snow.

Then she whispered it to Flake. "Amore to you, too!"

But she was supposed to be counting her happy times. Where was she?

That's right. She had managed to do five hundred skips with the skipping rope.

That was a record for her.

The whole class had stood and watched.

Then she was happy.

But she didn't have a best friend any more. Just other sorts of friends.

Like Jonathan and Vicky and Mickey. And Meatball. She liked him, too.

She was in an unusually well behaved class,
the teacher told Dani's father.

They didn't bounce off chairs or anything
like that.

But the teacher must have forgotten about
Benny—the boy who didn't want to start school
until his mother bribed him with money.

One time he crept out of the classroom and ran
to the candy store.

Then he crept back in again.

The teacher saw him though, and at playtime she gave him a serious talk.

No one knew what she said, but it didn't help. Benny kept on eating candy in school, even though it wasn't allowed.

And sometimes he lay on the floor and crawled around like a crocodile.

It usually ended with him having to sit next to the teacher at her desk.

But the best happy thing was…

The letter!

One day Dani got a letter. When she read it, she
was the happiest she'd been in her whole life.

Hello Dani! it said.
I can't live without you.
Love from Ella

And in the envelope was Ella's most special
bookmark, the angel.

Chapter 19

Dani answered right away.

Hi Ella!
You must try, until we grow up.
Then we can move to the same town and live in
the same house and have the same job.
We could work in the same shop.
Or we could cure sick animals in Australia or
Africa.

Love from Dani
PS Your town would also be okay.

Soon she got an answer:

Hi Dani!
I can't wait that long.
Can you visit me at Easter?
Love from Ella

And then a few days later Ella's mother called
Dani's father to ask if Dani could visit them.

Dani was going there in the morning.

Oh, she couldn't wait for the morning!

But that didn't mean time went any faster...

Snow and Flake were going, too.
At last they would meet Partyboy!

Chapter 20

Her father opened the door again.

"Dani, what are you doing?" he sighed. "Go to bed!"

He wanted to go to bed, too.

He was going to drive Dani the whole way.

"I'm so happy I can't sleep," she complained.

"I know a trick," said her father. "If you count sheep…"

"No, not sheep," said Dani. "That's boring."

"Count backwards then," her father suggested. "Count backwards from twenty!"

"Twenty, nineteen, eighteen…" Dani counted, but that didn't help either.

When she got to seventeen, she remembered a trick she had learned from her cousin Roseanna.

The trick was to close your eyes and pretend you were asleep.

Sometimes you fall asleep properly.

It worked!

Quick as a wink, Dani fell asleep.

And when she woke up it was morning and she was going to visit Ella.

That meant a new chapter would begin in Dani's happy life.